When the Light Fades and Other Stories

Victor Kabagi

Whitney Hope Wanjiku

Ukiyoto Publishing

All global publishing rights are held by

Ukiyoto Publishing

Published in 2023

Content Copyright © Victor Kabagi, Whitney Hope Wanjiku

ISBN 9789360167745

All rights reserved.
No part of this publication may be reproduced, transmitted, or stored in a retrieval system, in any form by any means, electronic, mechanical, photocopying, recording or otherwise, without the prior permission of the publisher.

The moral rights of the author have been asserted.

This is a work of fiction. Names, characters, businesses, places, events, locales, and incidents are either the products of the author's imagination or used in a fictitious manner. Any resemblance to actual persons, living or dead, or actual events is purely coincidental.

This book is sold subject to the condition that it shall not by way of trade or otherwise, be lent, resold, hired out or otherwise circulated, without the publisher's prior consent, in any form of binding or cover other than that in which it is published.

www.ukiyoto.com

I dedicate this work to my father, Thomas.

Acknowledgement

I would like to extend my sincerest thanks to the following people:

Whitney Hope Wanjiku for her immense encouragement to do this work.

Mitei Elisha, my English literature teacher who nurtured my love for writing.

Margaret, my aunt who supported me through advice and guidance.

My Aunt Rose Kabagi.

Contents

My Father's Military Life	1
When the light fades	12
The Smoke	17
About the Author	*24*

My Father's Military Life

I joined the army thirty years ago. I was twenty-five years old, with a well built, masculine body and young blood that worked to my advantage in running the military operations tactfully. Life was berries and thorns. Each day waking up to a different surprise operation. The best part of it all was the position I held in the team and the army at large. Given my swift and apt natured body, I was the best decorated sniper, the Impala Forces ever had, in the history of the *Banto* team.

A group of about thirty highly decorated men and a woman named *Q'S, which* translates to Quick Sense, was the best team I ever and mostly enjoyed working with. Q'S was sharp sensed and a think tank at the same time in our team. She carried out military operations skillfully and without any collaterals, the skill that saw her rise from one rank to another. Her living slogan was always one, "no one should be left behind."

"Father, are you talking to yourself?" asked Riya, his son.

"No, am just reminding myself of the hunting days", said the now retired first lieutenant Moli, now a grizzled old man.

"Did, I hear you say hunting? Perhaps you have forgotten everything lieutenant" said Riya jokingly, twitching his mouth a little.

"Have you been into the military yet?" he asked loudly, his voice carrying a certain finality of command. "No, not yet, but again I prefer to dare not, do you know why?" asked Riya, pulling his rocking chair to where the old man sat quietly, recalling the halcyon days in the field of combat.

"Maybe", he answered, raising his faint voice a little this time. His son looked straight into his eyes, which ranged from black to pale brown, still wondering why his father loved the military life with so much passion, then with a last glance at him, he said, "because even after hanging your boots, you still order me around loudly", before he left. "Once a soldier always one kid".

One evening while seated under a palm tree, Mr. Moli came and sat next to his son, Riya, but kept a considerable distance between them, just in case safety was needed. Despite his old age, Mr. Moli had a strong grip of his hands and they were still energetic. Perhaps, that is why his son kept distance between them.

"Son, he began. Being a soldier is not an easy task. First, your personal life is at stake, secondly, you have your team to cover, something that I once in my line of duty, failed to do and it really cost me.

"What did it cost you father?", interrupted his son.

"Just listen…I am coming to that son", this time he said avoiding his eyes.

We were in '*Operation Fox*'. My boss, who is now the serving First Lieutenant, had assigned us a deadly mission to rescue a certain minister's daughter. The operation was simple and everything in position, until the abductors raised an alarm that they were under attack. This was a secret mission and so no high authorities were informed about it, which meant no government support in form of backup or any aid was to be expected. I was their 'eye in the sky', on the pinnacle of a tall roof, about hundred meters from where the rescue mission was being undertaken. Then there was this lady…

"Which lady? Go on father…" Riya asked curiously, wanting to capture every detail into his tiny ears. Moli proceeded, assuming he had not heard the question. "So, this lady was covering the other soldiers, while I covered for her, from the roof top. My spotter rolled down the roof top, having been shot by the sniper from the abductor's side. So, I had to multi task. After I had spotted the abductors' sniper I released a shot killing him instantly but when I spotted this lady and zoomed her into position, I realized she needed urgent help. That's when I started shooting the abductors who were charging at her, before they could take her down.

"Father, who is this lady? Riya was curious to know her.

A soldier from my team", he answered angrily, probably because his son won't stop interrupting his narration.

"What was her name father?" he asked shyly, knowing his father was boiling angry and soon, he was going to lose his temper. Though he had been used to the military language and code, he had to control himself, since he was not in the active line of duty. "Her name is Q'S". He answered trying hard not to agitate him, before he proceeded with the narration.

"As I was saying, I had to multi task. I had to lead my team, cover my men and also the minister's daughter to protect, but the task was not that swift. Most of my men sustained serious injuries but worse of it all was the landmine that blew Q'S all the way up, drifting her in the air like a rudderless object. Though she was not that much hurt, I still felt I failed her, first, as her boss, commander, as a sniper and more so, as her close friend.

"Did she die? Asked Riya eyes popping out.

"I think I just said she wasn't that much hurt, did I?" he forwarded the answer to him. I think her super ability to sense, helped her a great deal, in evading the ferocious effect of that landmine. "What ability?", he asked.

"Q'S".

"What is Q'S?

Riya was becoming impatient to know everything.

"Quick Sense", he answered him proudly. This name reminded him of something special in his life, which he will always live to cherish.

"Is it someone's name?" he asked.

"Of course it is, why not?"

"I thought you said it is an ability, didn't you?

"Yes I did, but that is how we identified her from the team" he said smiling broadly.

Why father?

"Because they are military identification codes"

What was your code then?

"Well, uh, mine was the 'eye'

Wow! That is awesome! Said Riya convinced.

Of course it is son. Shall we proceed, or you are worn out?

"Go on lieutenant" Riya twitched a smile.

"Hey you! It is not lieutenant. It is retired First Lieutenant; do you understand?

"Yes, I get it" he said a little freaked this time.

No you don't. In military, we say, yes sir!

"Copy that"

Correct!

"Tell me about Q'S father" he said moving closer to the old man.

"She was beautiful and so is she till now and maybe, even to death. She was the best companion of my active service in the military."

He hesitated for a while, maybe to allow the information to sink deep into his son's head.

"Who was she? I mean her actual name father" he asked politely.

"Jessy Lihanda" he pronounced it very proudly.

"What!? What do you mean?" he asked, very shocked.

"That is it son" said the old man ignorantly.

"No, this can't be! How comes you never mentioned it to me all this time, huh? How comes she never mentioned her career to me?

You both betrayed my trust in you…he agitated furiously and gesticulated violently.

"Listen son, everything has its own time" he said unmoved by the madness that raged in his son's throat.

"Mother is very calm; her figure doesn't portray anything military. Her scar less faces and body, I mean, she is polite father, and not giving out orders like you do…" he vomited endless questions.

"Hey look here kid. Remember your mother was below me in rank. She took orders from me, and that is why she lives up to that obedience life she was used to, while in service, even after hanging her boots. That is who we are. Discipline is key my son…" he said chuckling.

"Why did she hung her boots, when she was supposed to be promoted? I guess you lured her into early retirement, right?"

"No, in fact, she is the one who convinced me into this perfect timing retirement!

"Why father?" he asked impatiently.

"We were from another deadly mission where we had escaped death by a whisker. She was badly hurt but fortunately, she recovered. Since she was my best soldier, I spent days watching and monitoring her, till she recovered. Despite having taken a bullet for her, I was discharged sooner than her. When she came back to her senses, the first thing she said was that she wanted immediate resignation from the force, which she was granted. Being her boss, and nearing retirement, I requested for an early one from the bosses and after clearance, I left for home. That is how Q'S and I met.

"Impressive story, but did mother recover fully?"

"Yes she did, and currently works as an undercover agent, with a private security company" said the old man, sipping a mouthful of *wimbi* porridge.

"Have you ever wondered or gave thought to the notion that, she might have been someone else's rose, but you still snatched her?" he asked persuasively. Moli, his father, sipped a few more mouthfuls before he could answer this pain in the ass but a true question, that demanded an urgent, legit and uncooked answer.

Well to be honest, most of my men, eyed on her. Given that she was the only woman in my team and with her apt and tactical skills to problem solving, otherwise known as 'think tank' in the military language, she was a beautiful, radiant gem, that everyone in the team longed to touch, feel, behold, love and protect at any cost. However, there was this barrier… he paused for a while to soften his dry lips and itchy throat.

"Which barrier Lieutenant?" He asked respectfully, trying to address him in the military language, as he referred to such.

"I said, re-ti-red, First Lieutenant! Not just Lieutenant! You have to go by the ranks. In the military, we do not like collaterals, ranks are paramount, you understand?"

"Yes Sir!" he yelled.

Now let me answer your question. As I told you earlier, she was senior Sergeant and all the other men took orders from her too and that explains why an ordinary soldier could not fall in love with their superior, first by age and another by rank. More so she had to portray a good military code of conduct and work be given the first priority over anything else; what you call peaceful coexistence and respect among employees and employers, as civilians.

"Oh! Now I see. That is why you eloped with this gem, right?

"Absolutely! Since I was the only option left, and the only one she was interested in." he said laughing loudly.

"But did it hurt you as a person to see that you broke the so-called code of conduct, by dating and marrying your soldier? I mean someone below your rank and in the line of work or duty as you call it?"

"Yes I admit to that, but there is something you are not getting son. Our relationship was purely professional, till that fateful day when she opened up to me about relationship and given the fact that I was three months to retirement, it was an added advantage that is why I requested for it, but for her case, it was between life and death. Her condition, required a quite longer period for her to recover fully and which is the reason, she was allowed to hang boots too, although she still gets her pensions wired to Western Union every month". He wipes tears of joy in his eyes.

"That is impressive. Do not cry, you are a buffalo soldier" he told him still laughing.

"I'm just happy for having got what I wanted best in my life son" he nods in contentment.

"Father, how comes she agreed to fall in love with you at that old age?" he inquired curiously.

"Your mother was in love, and so was I. Despite disparities in ages, it is very strong and it always breaks any barriers and boundaries and that is why we have lived happily together. More so, people meet despite what happens, only mountains don't.

"Yes father, you are right. I wish mother could hear this too". He said a bit emotional, hugging his father.

"That would be great because, she has been listening to this conversation all along from the start. Look, there she is." He said pointing to where Q'S, his beloved wife sat, tears of love and joy, welling down her red cheeks, as she witnessed a father son relationship and conversation. It was very lovely for her to witness such love, because it has always been her dream to see her family happy and living a fulfilled life. It was a dream come true!

She slowly walked to where her son and her husband sat, as their son Riya, ran to meet her.

They embraced each other then sat around a stark fire, still chatting about the military days. "So you heard everything?" Riya asked her a little perplexed.

"Yes son, I must say I am so proud of you and how you were asking those questions". She said caressing and kissing his forehead and cheeks.

"So you are the criminal here?". He asked her angrily.

"No! Why do you say so?". His mother asked a bit shocked at what was happening.

"You lured my father into marrying you, that was sabotage! He spurt furiously.

"No, it was true love my son. That is why we have you with us today; our only son, right daddy?". She answered fearfully.

"Ha! Ha! Ha! Look at who is scared to death, Ha! Ha! Ha! He laughed till his ribs ached. I wanted to see your reaction mother. I didn't know that even soldiers get emotional and frightened, Ha! Ha! Ha!

"Of course we do son." The two answered simultaneously, embracing their son.

"I want to say I love you both, so much. Both as biological and my military parents and I am so proud of you because you have convinced me into becoming a soldier someday". He said amidst tears.

"We love you too our son". His mother whispered.

"Father, thank you for taking me through your military life. I am fully convinced to join them some day". He said as they walked slowly back into the house for the night.

Wimbi brown porridge made from ground millet and sorghum.

When the light fades

"Supposing one day you leave us, where will you go?", asked Clara politely. "No! Can you listen to yourself?", interrupted Lana furiously. She never liked the idea that her mother was going to die. She was always ready to do anything to save her ailing mother from the sharp spikes of death, that were waiting for an opportune time to snatch her away from them. Andisi had been bedridden for five years. She knew not the day when she would 'close' her eyelids. She was skinny and emaciated like a sculpture of a dead dinosaur. Her back was stoop and legs bow shaped. Tears drizzled from the corners of her eyes nonstop like a permanent river.

Her lips, dry as crisp and cracked like gulley erosion, twitched a little when she saw her two poor daughters, seated beside her. Since they learnt about their mother's sickness, they always quarreled and fought due to disagreements about the difference in the ideas they gave. Their mother, Andisi, just stared blankly at them with pale white eyes from which hot pus-like tears welled down her grey cheeks. She wondered how her daughters would survive the next part of their journey in her absence. She envisaged the small piece of land they had, together with a small goat. First, they were too young to cultivate the land but old enough to look after their small goat.

The only house they had was one grass thatched hut, which sipped in water when it rained. They huddled themselves in a small corner of the hut due to the mud that accumulated during rainy season. However, during the dry season, they watched the sky and the moon from the comfort of their, hut, through a huge opening on the roof. A goat was the only valuable property they possessed together with a small piece of land which could not sustain them for long. Their grannies had long departed and so was their father.

Thomas, who was their father had died of heart inflammation due to his ever dutiful habit of excessive drinking of spirit. He was a grizzled old man who met their mother in the drinking spree. What transpired was a long tale to tell, but Andisi and Thomas fell in fantasy love and sired two beautiful, poor daughters. He died when Clara was four months old, leaving his wife the burden of parenting. Of Andisi's parents, it remained a mystery, though rumors had it that, they died of bone cancer and depression.

Clara and Lana just watched their mother in perplexity. When they saw their mother crying, they too joined her. It was very painful to imagine that their ever dutiful and loving mother was going to die and leave them lonely. "Mother do not leave us alone... please". Clara the younger one said caressing her mother's dry lips and hands. Lana who was the elder one, understood clearly that this was her mother's 'goodbye' to them. With a last glance at her daughters, she went mute, but her eyes remained open, tears flooding from them.

"Mother! Mother! Wake up, wake up please...", Cried Lana sorrowfully shaking her mother violently. Clara could not understand what was happening at that time. "Stop shaking her! Can't you see she is still alive?" Said Clara angrily, pushing her sister away. Lana could not believe her eyes. The person that they had been used to, all the years of their existence, was no more! Very painful." Mother is dead Clara "she answered her sister amidst sobs. "But how? Her eyes are open..." Clara thought her sister was pulling her leg, about their mother. This is when Lana moved closer to where her mother's lifeless body lay and closed her eyes. When Clara saw this, she accused her sister of having killed their mother, just because she closed her eyes. Lana knew very well that her mother had passed on, on her own but Clara could hear none of that. She said their mother was still talking to them but Lana, her sister could not argue with her and walked outside still sobbing bitterly. Clara let out a loud yell that saw neighbors and passersby flooding their small compound.

She explained everything to them and stood on her word that, her sister had killed their mother. Given the fact that she was the eldest, and was outside crying, everyone believed Clara's accusations, that Lana had indeed murdered their poor mother. When it was confirmed that Andisi's body was ice cold, they claimed it was a natural death but Clara insisted that she saw her sister touching their mother's eyes. When the onlookers looked keenly in Andisi's eyes and discovered they were pale, they seconded Clara's accusations without a second thought.

They claimed that Lana had bewitched her mother and that she should be cast out of the village. Andisi was buried in their small piece of land without much ado. They were pagans and so no one bothered to look for a priest. They just said, 'ashes to ashes and soil to soil', before her body was covered in red mound of soil. Their small goat was used for cleansing. It was painful to lose both a parent and a lifetime companion for Clara. She then recalled the question she asked her mother, "supposing one day you leave us, where will you go?", but her mother had died before she could answer her. Too late!

Having been cast out of the village, she cried bitterly about her blood sister's bitter betrayal and wrongful accusations. She had lost her trust and confidence. Although she was her younger sister, she swore, she will never forgive her for this. Months dragged by slowly, without hearing from her sister. Clara remained in their matrimonial hut, while Lana became a member of the ape family. She roamed all day and spent the night on tree tops, a behavior that was became her habit.

One fine day, after roaming the whole day, she drew near the river to suppress her thirst.

Coincidentally, they met on the same spot. Clara was worn out and so was she. Having sipped a few handfuls, Lana called out her sister but she dared not come closer. Lana knew her sister could not believe that she was innocent and so she said…" Clara, I am your sister, I did not kill our mother. She was already dead when I closed her eyes in order to honor her, but you thought I killed her. I accept to carry the blame for as long as it will take me, but I want you to know one thing; when the light fades, darkness engulfs the sky until truth manifests. I will be no more, I love you Clara. Now that I have seen you…" After this she dived into the fast moving water and away she was sweep!

"Did she say when the light fades? sister! Sister!" Instead of reply from her sister, it was her own echo that sounded back, "when the light fades, darkness engulfs until the truth manifests"." I will be no more".

The Smoke

The story was told of the famous four who reigned in the forlorn hearts of everyone who lived in the early '60's. The country had been under siege by the whites. African slavery had been abolished but not fully. The pre independence struggle which was constantly in the air, had claimed a lot of innocent and guilty lives of both the Africans and those of white colonialists altogether.

Rumors had it that, some of the African countries had earlier on gained independence and those who had no yet gained, fought tooth and nail, to achieve it. The smell of blood shed was everywhere. This really threatened the continued stay of the whites and their security at large. Masses of corpses were dumped daily on the banks of Sirikwa dam without someone to give them decent burials. The harsh colonial rule stated that Africans were wild animals who deserved no burial but be thrown out in the forest to rot or be devoured upon by other wild animals.

The famous four, will tell you, how survival for the fittest was key. The deadly struggle between the White's superior flame and the African's inferior clubs, clashed claiming more African lives compared to the settlers. Of the four that witnessed this, was Caril. A tall dark and masculine guy, whose chin was enclosed in a bushy moustache and large beard. His eyes were pepper red despite his ever polite nature. Caril's story was worse than everyone else's. His parents Mr. and Mrs. Chogo lived in Duran forest before the white settler's inversion.

Caril was a year old when the atrocities began. His mother had left for a distant forest to collect wood while his father was working in the settler farms, pruning and picking cotton every day. The white settlers had also taken charge of the wildlife and all the African wildlife sanctuaries that existed by then. Unfortunately, while collecting firewood, Caril's mother was caught and detained.

When Chogo, Caril's father, heard about his wife's arrest over trespass, he really got furious and very mad. The madness which led him to stabbing the supervising officer, in the chest, fourteen times. When the other guards discovered he was behind their senior's murder, he was sentenced to twelve years' imprisonment with hard labor in the tea plantations. Mr. Chogo's life became unbearable since the very day of imprisonment. First he was tattooed a huge monkey skeleton on his chest using a red hot iron rod. He cried out loudly and painfully as the iron rod sunk into his thick, masculine and succulent skin.

The other black prisoners watched in horror as their own endured the pain. From their looks, it was evident that 'enough was enough' and that such harassment and mistreatment was enough and should come to an end with immediate effect. Two weeks passed. Every day was weeping and whipping for him, accompanied by a whole truck of insults. His back turned into furrows of black flesh and streams of 'black blood'. The humiliations had become too much for him to bear.

Caril's mother, Sugut, on the other hand, was sentenced to ten days' imprisonment and five days of hard labor in coffee farm. She too underwent hardships from the guards, who called her all sorts of names, ranging from, "the mother of all apes", to the," last standing ancestor of apes". Despite this humiliations, she kept her mouth shut. She feared she might be killed and never to see her son again. Caril on his side was found by a hunter girl. It was after she saw a huge smoke in the forest and ran speedily to put it out before the guards could notice. She managed to arrive at the scene but when there she found a little boy, Caril being chocked by the smoke. She quickly grabbed him and off she ran away with him before the guards could arrive. That is how he was saved. Sugut, Caril's mother, was set free after her term was over. On her way home, she was shot in the head by the guards, who then after shooting her, laughed sarcastically saying, "no more mother gorilla".

Mr. Chogo was notified of his wife's death while in the bars. It was like adding salt to a raw injury that was too raw to probe. He never saw the need to live anymore. His life had become like a rudderless object being drifted in the air without a distinct direction. One night, of the fateful day, all prisoners lined up for food before they could be locked up again." I swear today over this food, that, we all die for a good course, in the pursuit of liberty and freedom... " said Mr. Chogo tearfully. All the other six hundred black prisoners repeated after him in a chorus. The guards thought it was a joke. It was midnight and behold the 'Grand monsoon prison' began to fume.

Thick clouds of smoke, lined up heading straight into the pitch black sky. All the African slaves, prisoners, white guards, cooks and everyone in the building that fateful night, was reduced to smoldering, hot, grey and black ash. Before the prisoners breathed their last, they left a short message which said; "we have sacrificed our lives for the nourishment of a promising tomorrow. We all feel pain, we all have blood and only skin color is different. Just like you hate our color, yours too, we hate. Respect and humanity are the elements that leads to love and peaceful coexistence. Tomorrow a new day will sprout!

It was truly painful for the Africans who had lost their loved ones in the 'Grand monsoon prison' fire. The following morning, news had spread everywhere about the massive 'human sacrifice' in the Grand monsoon prison, for the blacks. All the six hundred slaves and prisoners had perished, without forgetting the three hundred or so prison warders and guards, cooks, secretaries, the farm produce among others. It was a massive loss of property ever heard in the history of the white settler's stay in Africa.

The girl who took in Caril was Laur. She too had been displaced following the massive resettlement order.

She had gone playing with fellow kids in the nearby village, when the White paladin armies swarmed the village, torching everything grassy in their way. Huts were burned down. Those who were outside were lucky to be alive while those who were still inside, burned to ashes alive! The order was to resettle Africans in to the less productive lands to pave way for industrial revolution and urbanization. Laur was lucky to be alive, because were it not for the other kids to call her to accompany them to play, she would be no more.

The crops and everything green was torched leaving the soils bare. Cries of poor Africans filled the air with confusions everywhere. The scary Africans were caught between the rock and a hard place. Laur screamed loudly when she saw how her parents were being strangled to death by the thick cloudy smoke that suffocated them eventually. They died a painful death leaving a permanent scar in the lonely heart of Laur.

She sobbed uncontrollably till she passed out. The only thing she remembered was the misty smoke that emanated from their only hut, that was grass thatched. She brought with her two of her friends, Kalon and Kabagi. They faced constant hardships in trying to find life necessities, given the fact that their ages and mentality was still young. Only ten years later is when things began to click back into normalcy. They were adults, responsible to be exact and gifted differently. Laur was an exceptional cook. She made different recipes for the four of them every day, since their arrival in Param village.

Kabagi was an excellent hunter. He would bring home large chunks of buck meat and rabbit. There are some days when he brought antelope meat. Every day, food was in constant supply for the four of them. The food was stored in their grass thatched hut near the smoke for preservation. Caril on the other hand, was a gifted carpenter who used his natural ability to thatch lovely huts made from mud, poles and papyrus reeds. Sometimes he would use strong bamboo poles.

Kalon was a little girl whose abilities were incomparable. She was a skilled fighter who provided them security during the night and day. She would spend six long hours combing the forest, just to ascertain that nothing endangered their lives, not even a rattling snake. There was a day when she drilled a wolf's eyes out, alive! With her bare hands. She was also well gifted in weaving baskets. She would weave at least twenty baskets a day without any disturbances and at least twelve when there was minimal distraction. She sold the baskets in exchange of other valuable items like spears, arrows and bows.

She was also a silent girl, who spoke less and answered when asked. She had feelings for Kabagi so much, that she always spent most of her time near him. One day as they were seated around a stark fire outside, Caril asked a question no one was expecting; can you please tell us what you recall the last time you fled your village?

Laur was the first to answer. "I only recall the massive smoke that oozed from our hut, with my parents inside. It is the saddest moment ever and the long to forget memory in my entire life..." This she said tears drizzling down her pale cheeks. "As for me, I remember I was alone in the smoky hut, but before I could be choked to death, someone, probably a guardian angel, saved my life. I suppose it is you Laur, thank you so much." Caril said hugging her tightly, as they cried in each other's arms.

"I never saw my parents but the only thing that reminds me of them, is the cloudy smoke that I cannot remember well." Said Kabagi whispery, preventing himself from crying out loud. Kalon on the other hand, could not utter a word. She cried bitterly when she recalled how her parents were hanged and burnt alive, as she watched them struggle to free themselves in the acrid air of smoke. Kabagi moved closer to where she sat and embraced her. It remained a tale to tell of the painful deaths of smoke and mistreatment that they went through in the oppressive hands of the White rule, on their parent's behalf.

"Now that the smoke is all we know, let it reign in our forlorn hearts forever!" They said amidst sobs.

About the Author

Victor Kabagi

Kabagi is a seasoned authorwhose work has been recognized through his immense works of poetry, romance, thriller, short stories and Swahili works of tamthilia. Whitney is an upcoming author and this being her first piece of writing, she has been so elated in publishing it. Among those books authored by Victor Kabagi includes: African Whispers, Tentacles of Love, The Smoke, Unquenchable Tears, The Killer Coin among others. Kabagi Victor is currently an automotive engineer. Whitney is an English Literature student at a recognized University in Kenya.

www.ingramcontent.com/pod-product-compliance
Lightning Source LLC
LaVergne TN
LVHW041601070526
838199LV00046B/2086